Usborne
Little First Stic[kers]

Seashore

Illustrated by
Stephanie Fizer Coleman

Words by Jessica Greenwell
Designed by Maddison Warnes

Expert advice from Dr. John Rostron
and Dr. Margaret Rostron

You'll find all the
stickers at the back
of the book.

Along the seashore

Put another
boat in the sea.

Add some sandcastles
to the beach.

At the rock pool

Stick all sorts of
sea creatures in
the rock pool.

Add some more
barnacles to the rocks.

Stick on some
more mussels.

5

Starfish and anemones

Stick lots of starfish in the
water and on the rocks.

Add some more
beadlet anemones.

On the rocks

Stick lots of crabs in
the rock pool.

Put some topshells and
periwinkles in the water.

Diving birds

Stick on some flying cape gannets.

Add a cape cormorant resting on the rocks.

8

Fill the water with sea birds
diving for herring.

Seals and seal pups

Add some little seal
pups to the picture.

Find a place for
a diving seal.

10

Puffins and pufflings

Stick some more
puffins in the sky and
on the rocks.

Stick on some more pufflings
snug in their burrows.

Sea otters

Stick on lots more
swimming otters.

Find a place for an otter diving for a sea urchin.

Add some more sea urchins.

13

Penguins and chicks

Add some Magellanic penguins to the rocks.

Stick on a rockhopper penguin jumping into the water.

Add some more little
penguin chicks to the picture.

Fill the water with some more swimming penguins.

Sea turtles

Stick the Moon and some more stars in the sky.

Add more turtles leaving the sea to lay their eggs in the sand.

Along the seashore pages 2-3

Seagulls

Windsurfer

Boat

Seagulls

Curlews

Shore crabs

Bucket

Sandcastles

Rock pool

Ball

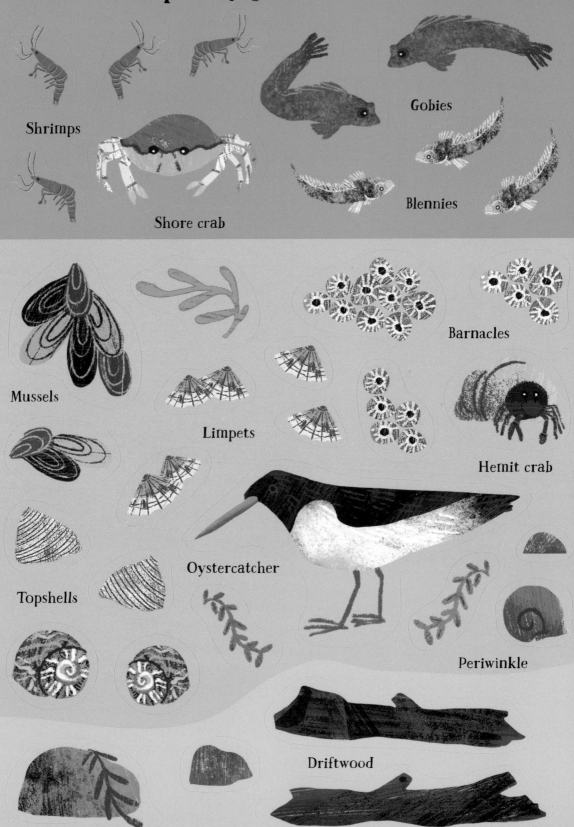

At the rock pool

Shrimps

Gobies

Shore crab

Blennies

Mussels

Barnacles

Limpets

Hemit crab

Topshells

Oystercatcher

Periwinkle

Driftwood

Starfish and anemones page 6

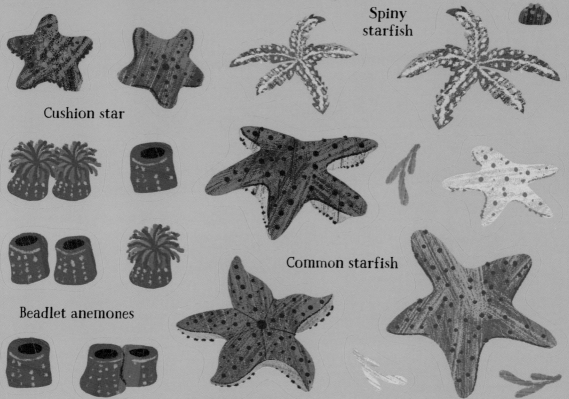

Spiny starfish

Cushion star

Common starfish

Beadlet anemones

On the rocks page 7

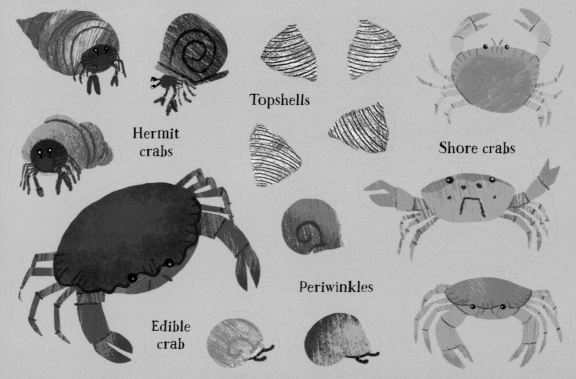

Hermit crabs

Topshells

Shore crabs

Periwinkles

Edible crab

Diving birds pages 8–9

Cape
cormorant

Cape
gannets

Herring

Seals and seal pups page 10

Seals

Seal pups

Puffins and pufflings page 11

Puffins

Pufflings

Sea otters pages 12-13

Floating otter
holding a sea urchin

Sea otters

Kelp
crabs

Garibaldi
fish

Sea
urchins

Penguins and chicks pages 14-15

Rockhopper
penguins

Magellanic
penguins

Penguin chicks

Sea turtles page 16

Olive Ridley
sea turtles

Moon and
stars

You can use these stickers anywhere.